More books about Kipper:

Kipper
Kipper's Birthday
Kipper and Roly
Kipper's Monster
Kipper's Beach Ball
Kipper's Snowy Day
Kipper's Christmas Eve
Hide Me, Kipper!
One Year with Kipper
Kipper's A to Z
Kipper Storyboards
First Kippers
Kipper Story Collection

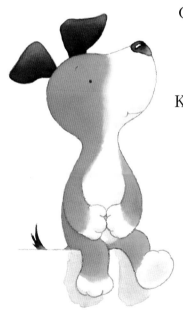

First published in 1992
by Hodder Children's Books

This edition published in 2008

Text and illustrations copyright © Mick Inkpen 1992

Hodder Children's Books
338 Euston Road
London NW1 3BH

Hodder Children's Books Australia
Level 17/207 Kent Street
Sydney, NSW 2000

A catalogue record of this book is available
from the British Library.

ISBN: 978 0 340 93207 0
10 9 8 7 6 5 4

Printed in China

Hodder Children's Books is a division of
Hachette Children's Books.
An Hachette UK Company.

www.hachette.co.uk

What any author wants is for his books to become dog-eared and familiar. I've been lucky enough that my very young readers are particularly adept at giving their books doggy ears in no time at all.

And of all my books, perhaps it's those about Kipper that get the doggiest ears of all, which I guess is kind of appropriate.

Mick Inkpen

Kipper's Toybox

Mick Inkpen

*Hodder
Children's
Books*

A division of Hachette Children's Books

Someone or something had been nibbling a hole in Kipper's toybox.

'I hope my toys are safe,' said Kipper. He emptied them out and counted them.

'One, two, three, four, five, six, SEVEN! That's wrong!' he said. 'There should only be six!'

Kipper counted his toys again.
This time he lined them up to
make it easier.

'Big Owl one, Hippopotamus two,
Sock Thing three, Slipper four,
Rabbit five, Mr Snake six.'

'That's better!' he said.

Kipper put his toys back in the toybox. Then he counted them one more time, just to make sure.

'One, two, three, four, five, six, seven, EIGHT NOSES! That's two too many noses!' said Kipper.

Kipper grabbed Big Owl and threw him out of the toybox.

'ONE!' he said crossly.

Out went Hippopotamus, 'TWO!'

Out went Rabbit, 'THREE!'

Out went Mr Snake, 'FOUR!'

Out went Slipper, 'FIVE!'

But where was six? Where was Sock Thing?

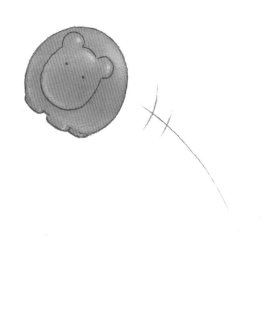

Kipper was upset. Next to Rabbit, Sock Thing was his favourite. Now he was gone.

'I won't lose any more of you,' said Kipper. He picked up the rest of his toys and put them in his basket. Then he climbed in and kept watch until bedtime.

That night Kipper was woken by a strange noise.

It was coming from the corner of the room.

Kipper turned on the light. There, wriggling across the floor, was Sock Thing! It must have been Sock Thing who had been eating his toybox!

Kipper was not sure what to do. None of his toys had ever come to life before. He jumped back in his basket and hid behind Big Owl.

Sock Thing wriggled slowly round in a circle and bumped into the basket. Then he began to wriggle back the way he had come.

He did not seem to know where he was going. Kipper followed.

Quickly Kipper grabbed him by the nose. Sock Thing squeaked and wriggled harder.

Then a little tail appeared. A little pink tail.

And a little voice said, 'Don't hurt him!'

So it was YOU! You have been making the hole in my toybox!' said Kipper.

It was true. The mice had been nibbling pieces of Kipper's toybox to make their nest.

'You must promise not to nibble it again,' said Kipper.

'We promise,' said the mice.

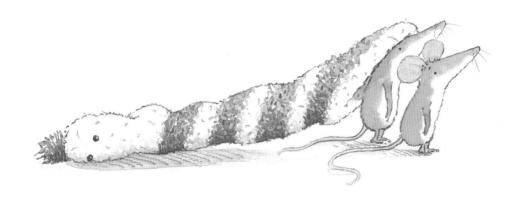

In return Kipper let the mice share his basket. It was much cosier than a nest made of cardboard and the two little mice never nibbled Kipper's toybox again...

B ut their babies did.
They nibbled EVERYTHING!

'My children absolutely LOVE all of Mick Inkpen's books, and I still love reading Kipper to them, even when it's for the hundredth time...'

CRESSIDA COWELL

'He is the perfect pup to grow up with...'

HILARY McKAY